FIRST JOB

"Kathleen!" I screamed, as I watched the wolfhound gallop down the hill we had just climbed up. "You're a bad girl!"

"And you are a shrill little girl," said a voice beside me that frightened me so I nearly—well, you can guess what I nearly. But I didn't. I just slowly unfroze my neck and turned enough to see who spoke, and there was the dragon, Mrs. Winchendon Livermore herself, breathing noisily through her highly arched nostrils, her chest rising and falling in beastly heaves, and I stood there waiting to be scorched by her wrath like Bradford Beeman and Mr. Tilley and poor Ernie Tellerman would have been if I hadn't been brave enough to take their places. . . .

GEORGINA AND THE DRAGON
was originally published by
Houghton Mifflin Company.

Critics' Corner:

"Spirited ten-year-old Georgina Gooch solves the dilemma of whether to attend the Commemorative Stamp Issue ceremonies in honor of her suffragist great-grandmother or her sister's wedding, upsets stereotyped ideas about sex roles in her family and town, and persuades a cantankerous old woman newspaper owner to start a paper recycling business. . . . The story is written with zest and humor and women liberationists as well as children will cheer the heroine's forthright attitudes toward people and situations."

—*A.L.A. Booklist*

". . . the amusing story is deftly written and would provide a good consciousness-raising experience for upper-elementary school girls and boys."

—*Library Journal*

About the Author and Illustrator:

LEE KINGMAN lives in Cape Ann, Massachusetts, with her husband and two children, where she leads a busy life writing books as well as managing a household. She is a member of the Horn Book Magazine Council and is editor of various volumes about the children's book field published by Horn Book, Inc. Among her many books for young people are *The Year of the Raccoon* and *The Peter Pan Bag*. Lee Kingman was born in Reading, Massachusetts, and graduated from Smith College. She had a career in publishing before she began to raise a family and to write on a full-time basis. In her spare time, Ms. Kingman enjoys designing, carving, and printing textiles on a press in her basement.

LEONARD SHORTALL was born in Seattle, where he attended the University of Washington. He now lives in New York City and is a well-known illustrator of books for boys and girls.

LEE KINGMAN

GEORGINA and the DRAGON

**Illustrated by
Leonard Shortall**

AN ARCHWAY PAPERBACK
POCKET BOOKS • NEW YORK

GEORGINA AND THE DRAGON

Houghton Mifflin edition published 1971

Archway Paperback edition published March, 1974
3rd printing .... July, 1976

Published by
POCKET BOOKS, a division of Simon & Schuster, Inc.,
A GULF+WESTERN COMPANY
630 Fifth Avenue, New York, N.Y. 10020.

Archway Paperback editions are distributed in the
U.S. by Simon & Schuster, Inc., 630 Fifth Avenue,
New York, N.Y. 10020, and in Canada by Simon &
Schuster of Canada, Ltd., Markham, Ontario, Canada.

For the Thought-Provokers

Suzi
Sue and Margaret
Barby, Judy—and Fritz

GEORGINA and the
DRAGON

My NAME is Georgina Gooch and it's not the name I would have picked for myself. In the first place it's a second-hand name. That is, George would be first-hand, and could I help it if my parents wanted a boy? They tell me I'm named for a great-grandmother who was famous, but she didn't like being a second-hand boy either. In fact she made it very clear. But when I said to my father, "How would you like it if your name was Thomasina?" he said, "Oh, Georgie! You're funny. My ears are too big." What kind of an answer is that? I'll tell you what kind. It's the kind I always get from my father.

I'm ten years old and I'd like to be called Gina. But try and break a habit, as my parents always tell me when I forget and chew on my hair. My parents started calling me Georgie as soon as they gave my name to be put on my birth certificate, along with that naked pink footprint. If I refer to myself as Gina, or get my friends to phone and ask for Gina, they ask, "Who?" and then yell, "It's for you, Georgie."

It's especially awful when you have four older sisters and they got the good names: Christine, Cheryl, Cynthia, and Charlene. Beautiful, right? Although you say them all at once in a hurry and it sounds like chewing celery. I also have a younger sister. Mother named her. My father nicknamed her. She's five and called Looey, because that's what happens to a name like Louisa around here.

I wonder if they use blue ink for baby boys' footprints on birth certificates. I asked my father, and he said, "At this rate we'll never know," and I asked, "Why?" and he said, "It's retribution."

So I asked my mother if Daddy had a serious illness, because he said having no boys was caused by retribution, and she said, "No, it's a matter of chromosomes. But he blames your great-grandmother, Georgina Poindexter Farraday."

"What was the matter with her—besides her name?"

"She was an insufferable suffragist!" roared

my father. "She worked so hard for Women's Rights not a boy has dared to be born in one generation of your mother's family since. Her name really was Georgina Poin*jinx*ter Farraday, that's what it was."

And that's when my mother quietly said, "It's too bad you feel that way about women," and stopped darning his socks and ironing his handkerchiefs. But she said even more quietly to me, "I let your father choose all your older sisters' names. Of course, he kept hanging hopefully onto Thomas MacIlwaine Gooch the Fourth, and when he couldn't use it on you, he gave up, and finally asked what I'd like to name a girl. So I said Georgina, because I figured you'd need all the inspiration and spunk from it you could get."

"What's spunk?" I asked, because it's a word I'm not used to hearing in today's world. Punk, yes. But not with an *s* in front of it, which sounds worse. I am very word conscious.

"Raw courage," said my mother. "That's what spunk is."

So you see what my problem is, being expected to have spunk in spite of myself and my great-grandmother.

The worst of it is, did you know she's going to be on a postage stamp? Next month. It's

3

a commemorative for Women's Rights. The seventy-fifth anniversary of the Georgina Poindexter Farraday March, and the one-hundredth anniversary of the year of her birth.

"What's so great about that?" I asked. "People are always having marches. Even the Little League," I added for my father's benefit. We all try to bring him into our conversation.

"Well, it was *great* in eighteen ninety-six in Idaho. She marched all the way from her home in Horse Shoe Bend to Boise in high button shoes and carrying a placard."

That was when I got my first faint twitch of admiration for her. Carrying things, like even the Brownie troop flag when I was younger, is hard after a while. Especially if your feet hurt, and high button shoes would be really miserable to hike in, particularly up and down those mountains in Idaho.

"What did it say on the placard?"

"You may well ask," groaned my father.

"It said VOTE IN BOISE FOR THE WOMAN'S VOICE——WOMEN ARE HERE FOR EVER," explained my mother. "She wasn't any poet, rhyming Boise and voice that way, but she did get to be known as Georgina Poindexter Farraday, Pioneer and Woman Forever."

4

"She was also known as the 'Noisy Lady Who Went to Boise,'" said my father.

"But she and her Noisy Boises won women the vote in the six-year-old state of Idaho in eighteen ninety-six," said my mother. "And that was quite an accomplishment."

We found out about the commemorative postage stamp because some man who was going to design it had written my mother to find out if we had any pictures of Georgina Poindexter Farraday where she wasn't wearing glasses and looking grim. Only he didn't dare say grim. He pretended he wanted a more relaxed feminine look for her and did we have any old informal snapshots where she looked as if she were having a good time?

"He's unhappy about putting WOMEN FOR-EVER over a face like that," my father sympathized.

I think that was the night we all had TV dinners, because Mother was very tired from cleaning the attic and composing a reply: "I am sorry to report that all my grandmother's pictures show her wearing glasses and looking intent. She always liked to see where she was going. Forever yours, Eve Merriweather Gooch."

We didn't hear any more for a while because

commemorative stamps are suggested by congressmen and committees, and we live in Ohio, not Idaho, so it wasn't our congressman, and my mother was always very good about committees. She never offered to be on one. She just waited to be asked, and she would only join a committee that met on Tuesday night or Thursday night. That was because my father bowled Tuesdays and played poker Thursdays. Mondays, Wednesdays, Fridays, Saturdays, and Sundays she stayed home in case he wanted to take her out. After all, once Christine was old enough, she had a line of instant baby sitters. But Father usually said after a hard day's work, he didn't need to go out—except for bowling and poker, even though my mother said after a hard day's work, she did. Need to go out. And of course Saturdays and Sundays he spent watching whatever was the sport of the season on TV.

But you've probably heard the same kind of discussions going on around your house, even if you don't have five sisters.

What we did was, we just went ahead and lived our own lives around him. Until the summer I'm writing about when my tenth birthday came in June and my oldest sister Christine announced she was going to be married on August the twentieth, and everyone except my father went into ecstasies and frenzies. He went into an economic depression. Deep. It worried me so much I learned the names of all the Cleveland Indians so I could communicate with him.

My sister Christine is efficient. She had the invitations engraved and addressed and ready to mail by the middle of July, and the very day she put them in the mail a letter arrived from the ladies of the Georgina Poindexter Farraday March Commemorative Stamp Issue Committee, inviting my mother and me, because of that name, to be present at the First-Day-Cover and Stamp-Selling Ceremonies in Boise, Idaho, on Friday, the twentieth of August.

"Well, I guess you won't be able to go galloping off to that!" said my father.

"No," said my mother sadly. "But one of us should. We'll send Georgie."

"A ten-year-old girl all alone!" my father protested.

"But I'm going to be a bridesmaid," I yelled. "I'm all measured for my gown!"

"Somebody should represent the family since they were kind enough to ask us to such an important occasion," said my mother. "Besides, you'll have other opportunities to be a bridesmaid."

"That's right. With my luck I'll be the bankrupt father of the bride at least four more times," my father sighed.

"Who's not getting married?" I asked logically.

"What do you mean?"

"There's six of us and you're only planning on five weddings."

"I'm glad you're good at math," said my father. "That's a happy surprise among seven women, all of whom can spend but none of whom can add. Tell me, just tell me, which one of you is out there earning anything and adding it and saving it? Not one of you. I'll drop dead before the last of you grows up and gets married."

That's the night I noticed my mother ironing his handkerchiefs again. She decided to save on tissues.

But I began to think about it and I really got worried. My father had a lot of problems. The next day I went out to get a job and do you know? It's practically impossible for a ten-year-old girl to get a job even if she's strong and tall!

Actually it wasn't fair of my father to say that none of us earned any money. We just didn't give any of it to him. My older sisters had a monopoly on the baby-sitting jobs in the neighborhood. My mother said she could start an agency

as soon as Looey learned how to write down phone numbers and messages. Looey could be the answering service because she already loved talking on the phone, and Mother would be the management and consultant. Consultant for emergencies like when Cheryl was sitting for the Lickdycker kids and they locked her in the bathroom. Then they took off all their clothes and began running around their yard. My mother saw them out the window. She knew Cheryl was too smart to let them out in March in Ohio with no clothes on, so she figured Cheryl wasn't in command of the situation, and Cheryl was usually in command of the situation, the telephone, or the bathroom. My mother hung up as soon as the Lickdyckers' phone had rung ten times and nobody answered. Then she called the fire department. The Lickdycker kids were so excited when the fire trucks all came that they wouldn't tell where the key was hidden, and the guys on the hook and ladder truck hauled Cheryl out a second-floor window.

But my father didn't consider baby-sitting as work, so if I wanted to impress him, that was out. I tried Mrs. Barberry next door about mowing her lawn, and she said, "Oh, Georgie, I have a boy to do that."

I asked Colonel Maypole, who's retired, if

he needed anyone to help him pot his plants or water them in the big greenhouse he calls his hobbyhouse, and he said, "Sorry, Georgie, I've got a man to do that. Mr. Tilley stokes the furnace night and morning and checks the temperature and the humidity, and when he's not doing that or weeding he plays horseshoes or checkers with me. Except on Thursdays—that's his day off. But I don't think you could do any of those things, do you?"

I think I could. Every day of the week. But he didn't give me a chance, even when I said I'd bring my jackstones as a change from horseshoes and checkers for him.

I asked Mrs. Vermeers, who lives in a wheelchair, mostly on her screen porch in summer, if I could do errands at the store for her, and she said, "Sorry, Georgie, I've got a boy with a car to do those for me."

Miss Finnerty had a boy to paint her front fence, and Miss Witherspoon had a young man to cut her hedge with the electric shears, for silly's sakes. She said, "Georgie, knowing you, you'd short-circuit yourself and I wouldn't want to be responsible."

I came home and said it sure was a man's world. Women didn't get equal employment opportunities at all.

"You can say that again," said Cynthia. "We can baby-sit and clean for pay before we get married, and then we can still baby-sit and clean for free after we get married."

"I'm not going to get married," I decided.

"That's a silly thing to say!" said Christine, who was all excited because she'd just received her first wedding present. We stood around while she unpacked it as carefully as if it were a bomb, and all it turned out to be was a pop-up toaster that didn't pop when she tried it. So she listed it under both her "thank yous to write" and her "things to return" columns.

She was calmer than my father, who was upset because his partner in the business had sent his daughter a toaster that didn't work. "Don't take it personally," Christine kept telling him. "Margie Perkins got five toasters and only two of them worked. You just don't *expect* things to work and then when they do, it's a nice surprise."

"But what do I say when Len asks me how you liked the toaster?"

"Just tell him the design is terrific. Tell him whoever picked it out, he or his wife, has terrific taste."

"Actually I think it was Sharon, our secretary, who picked it out," said my father

thoughtfully. "She does most of our errands for us."

Maybe I could be somebody's secretary and do their errands, I thought. But if I don't get married, I might be a secretary for the rest of my life—so why start now? Besides, typing letters and running errands could be a very boring way to spend your life. Almost as boring as running errands like my mother does all the time.

"Now we've settled the toaster problem," my mother said. "What shall I do about this invitation to the First-Day-Cover and Stamp-Selling Ceremonies in Boise? I have to answer it, and I can't go, but Georgie could."

"What are we going to do? Send her out by parcel post and have them plank a few sheets of Georgina Poindexter Farraday stamps over her and cancel her and mail her back?" asked my father, being humorous.

But my mother didn't think it was funny. "Don't you think our Georgina is capable of flying out and back by herself—*on an airplane, Thomas*—and being met by a lady from the committee, who would take care of her and see her through the ceremonies and put her on a plane to come back?"

"What ceremonies?" I asked, because the

only ceremonies I'd ever been to were my uncle's wedding and Christine's and Cheryl's high school graduations. "What sort of ceremonies could they have about licking some stamps and pounding them onto some letters because the glue isn't always so good?"

"They just wanted us to accept a sheet of stamps and say a few words and hand-stamp the first few special covers," said my mother, talking as if she'd saved stamps and known about first-day-cover collectors all her life—not just for the last week since the letter came and she called Colonel Maypole to find out what a first-day cover was. He said, "It's an envelope mailed from the place a new stamp is issued, with that stamp on it, and canceled on the date of its issue. Collectors send self-addressed envelopes to the postmaster ahead of time, and he takes care of stamping them and mailing them back. Some people try to collect every one that comes out in the U.S.A., and some people just collect special once-in-a-lifetime ones—like the moon-shot ones. I sure wish I had the first one canceled on the moon. That one will probably be the biggest collector's item of all times," he predicted.

Then my father had a thought. "Couldn't they just send you the stamps?" he asked my mother. "Maybe they'd even send them now and you could give them to Christine. She's running up a real postage bill here."

"That's hardly the point," said my mother.

"Bill!" gasped my father, and we all knew he meant money because there wasn't anyone named Bill in sight. "Who's paying for Georgie to fly from Ohio to Idaho? The U.S. Postal Service, the Committee for the Georgina Poindexter Farraday March Commemorative Stamp Issue First-Day Ceremonies, or Thomas Mac-Ilwaine Gooch the Third?"

"It's not quite clear," hedged my mother. "I'll just write and explain why I can't come and then just see what they suggest about Georgie."

"No one is consulting me," I complained. "Before you ask them what they suggest about my coming, you ought to ask me if I want to be going."

"Well, which do you want to do? To go or to be a member of the wedding?"

Everyone looked at me and it was quite unnerving because in a family of six girls you get used to all kinds of stares when people see you together in a family bunch, but you don't often have the experience of the whole group staring at one time and just focusing on you.

"I don't know—yet," I said. "Of course I

want to be a bridesmaid, but if all I had to do was say thank you and stamp some envelopes and I got a trip to Idaho out of it, I'd like to do that, too. You wouldn't mind too much, would you, Christine, if it turned out that I wasn't here? I might as well get something out of the name Georgina Poindexter Farraday Gooch."

"It's up to you, Georgie," she said, being hurt but noble. "You should do whichever will mean the most to you."

How's that for being put on a spot! As if I were a defector from the family instead of suddenly a distinguished member of it.

"I think this will solve itself very easily, Eve," said my father in his business voice. "You just write your letter and explain you can't come and your husband isn't about to pay for plane fare across the country so his ten-year-old daughter can hand-cancel some envelopes with his grandmother-in-law's picture on them labeled WOMEN FOREVER."

"Yes, dear," agreed my mother. "I'm quite sure the ladies will understand the situation—only too well."

So my father said, "That's that," and took his bag with his bowling shoes and special bowling ball and left.

Maybe I'm not giving you a fair picture of my

19

father. After all, a man who has seven women in his household must yearn for male company, and also I suppose he has a right to feel Women's Lib is all out of proportion—from his point of view. But I did begin to wish he saw me as me, Georgina Gooch, instead of as just one of his many daughters, or just another girl. After all, I was Georgina Poindexter Farraday's great-granddaughter and namesake, and I was beginning to feel that had to be special whether I got to Idaho or not. I was going to have to make something of it.

The next day my mother sent me out to mail her letter to the committee, and the nearest mailbox was two blocks down the street. She stopped to take a good look at me before I went out and she sighed. I'm no tomboy. I don't fight, bite, or scratch, talk dirty, or hassle little kids. And I don't climb trees and get way out on the top limbs and scream with fright either. I just stick to the lower branches. I don't like getting hit with a dodge ball or having to spank a volleyball back hard over the net at school. But I don't think I'm better than boys right now because I'm taller or smarter. Live and let live, that's my motto. No hassle.

But when my mother shook her head and sighed, I knew why. I'm plain. The other girls got the looks—black shiny curly hair and big blue eyes and pink cheeks and even teeth that look like those in ads. I'll bet even Looey's front teeth grow in straight, although she's just hoping they grow in for the wedding. But I've got limp brown hair, and green eyes if I wear green, and muddy eyes if I wear blue, and glasses and crooked teeth, and I'm not aggressive. At least it said so on my sixth grade year-end report, which my mother stuck in her underwear drawer before my father could take offense at it—she knew he couldn't stand one more woman telling him what to do: "Georgina has not lived up to her mental potential this year. Her ego-confidence needs reinforcement at home and among her peers. May I suggest her father put aside but one hour a week to devote to Georgina exclusively and bring her out of her shell? Perhaps if he took her bowling or found some activity they could share and build a more meaningful relationship together it would help to correct her timidity and unwillingness to participate in sports and other group activities. Sincerely, Miss Brockelmeyer."

If Miss Brockelmeyer had asked me, I could have told her my whole life at 262 Maple Drive was a group activity, my unwillingness to participate in sports would be totally reinforced by having to bowl with my father, and my timidity is simply reserve. But I guess you look at me and don't see anything—not looks like my sisters', nor mental potential like my mother had when she gave up her research job on rat psychology to get married, and you just don't see me looking at you and trying to figure you out. That's my reserve.

Anyway my mother for once didn't say, "Georgie, for heaven's sakes, stand up straight," when she sent me off to mail the letter. My father always reminded me by saying, "Boys don't like girls who walk around looking like pretzels."

I won't go into Father's other manly observations that always irk my mother. She usually just says, "I know you particularly feel absolutely dominated by the female sex, and I'm sorry about that. But it would be a relief if men took women's *minds* into consideration for a change. That's what my grandmother said in eighteen ninety-six and we shouldn't seventy-five years later still be trying to have that basic factor understood."

"Well," said my father thoughtfully, "if it was your minds you wanted to be admired for, you had a better chance of making the point in eighteen ninety-six than you do in nineteen seventy-one. And since the idea didn't take hold then, I don't think you've got a chance now."

"Why not?" asked my mother with considerable indignation.

"Because about all a man could plainly see of a woman in eighteen ninety-six was her head, which should have called attention to her mind all right. But since then—Wow!"

That was when my mother said for me to take Looey and go mail that letter. Fortunately Looey wanted to stop in the next yard and play with Mrs. Barberry's kittens and Mrs. Barberry said she didn't mind. So I had a rare chance to be alone and think all the way to the mailbox and I mailed the letter and I sat down on Colonel Maypole's steps up to his brick front walk to think some more. It was cool and shady because he had a big maple tree on his front lawn, and it was quiet for thinking, except I wasn't sure what I was trying to decide. And then it crept up on me. I really wanted to have an adventure and go to Idaho and I'd come back and write it up and be a reporter and sell the story to the local paper and I'd have a career as a newspaperwoman and a writer. I wanted to do something with my brains. I couldn't help remembering my mother after three weeks of bad weather and everyone having the flu lying down while she had it standing up, looking at all the laundry that had piled up and saying, "And to think I gave up a career in rat psychology—for this!"

But if the U.S. Postal Service or the Committee for the Georgina Poindexter Farraday March Commemorative Stamp Issue First-Day Ceremonies wasn't planning on paying my way, and my father wasn't, how was I going to get there to start my career? I had fifteen dollars in my bank account, and as I said, the job situation for girls was discouraging.

When Bradford Beeman threw his bike down on Colonel Maypole's steps and just missed conking me with the handlebar, I asked, "Why don't you look where you're going, and what's the matter?" because Bradford Beeman is very careful of his things. You'd usually think his bicycle was gold-plated the way he stops and parks it and puts down the kickstand. For him to hurl his bike down that way, something had to be hassling him.

"I'm going to give up this paper route, that's what's wrong, Georgie. It's not worth the money to have Mrs. Livermore yelling at me every day I deliver the paper—and then practically make me get down on my knees and beg to be paid each week."

24

"Mrs. Livermore is the old lady who lives on the hill?"

"Right. It's way out of my way to take the paper up there anyway. So I told her today I wouldn't deliver it anymore and she said in that case, she'd have the sales manager fire me. It seems she owns the paper. But I can't quit. I'm saving for an electronic computer building set."

"Mmhhmmmm," I said, beginning to feel an idea. You know how boys pretend to drive motorcycles and go "Va-Room, Va-Room, VA-ROOM!" Well, that's the way an idea starts in my mind, with a vibration that shakes loose that va-va-va noise. I knew something was coming, but I didn't know what.

Bradford sat there beside me, too shaken even to go collect from Colonel Maypole, who never yelled at anyone, and along came Ernie Tellerman, who is clever. He thought up the dog-walking idea around town and usually he's pretty cool as he strolls by on his job, even when he's trying to untangle two poodles, a cocker spaniel, and a dachshund and their leashes. I've heard him say, "No harder than working Howdy Doody's strings."

But right now he looked as if he'd just been in a dog fight, and I shouldn't have said, "Along came Ernie Tellerman." There went Ernie Tel-

lerman, skidding like a water-skier about to get ditched and being towed by the most enormous dog I've ever seen in my whole life. Sweat was flying off Ernie's forehead and the dog that was pulling him kept up a steady gallop that could have won Ernie a track record over the high hurdles.

"Help!" gasped Ernie. "This creature's killing me."

I could see the dog was about to tackle the traffic and while cars would try to avoid his denting their fenders, they might not see it was a package deal, with Ernie coming on behind now like a drag chute trying to slow the dog down.

Bradford still had his mouth open, muttering, and his bike was lying practically in my lap, so I jumped up and hopped on it and tried to pass the dog and head him into the shrubbery at the edge of Colonel Maypole's yard. As I pedaled past Ernie I could see he'd made the mistake of winding the leash around his wrist and he was stuck with it.

"What's the dog's name?" I asked, and with about his last gasp, Ernie said, "Kathy! And don't run over her. She's *extremely valuable*."

Kathy was a silly name for a great awkward dog like that— all chest and legs, and feet like roller skates. But as you know, people are not always thoughtful about names.

I was just about at the dog's ear level as I crammed the bike past her on the sidewalk, so I leaned toward her and said with stern command, "Kathy, cool it. Stop. Halt. Sit. Stay." Our neighbor Mr. Broderick had taken his boxer to obedience school and I used to hear him practice in his backyard. His boxer got to be very relaxed about watching Mr. Broderick stay.

Maybe Kathy was tired. Maybe she knew what "sit" meant. Anyway, she sat suddenly while I pedaled right into Colonel Maypole's barberry hedge, and Ernie Tellerman lay fulllength on the sidewalk. I was screeching about my scratches from the barberry thorns and Bradford was screeching about the scratches on his bike's orange Day-Glow fluorescent paint job and Ernie was breathing and just about able to turn his head away from Kathy, who was licking him with a tongue as big as a washcloth.

But in a minute or two Bradford and I sat down beside Ernie on the sidewalk and Bradford got his Scout knife out and cut the leather leash before Ernie could stop him.

"Mrs. Livermore's not going to like that," groaned Ernie. "But I don't care. I'm going to quit. If she wants to exercise an Irish wolfhound called Champion Mavourneen, Kathleen of Connacht, she can do it herself."

So Kathy was short for a fancy champion name as well as being one of the biggest dogs possible. Just sitting on the sidewalk, she could look right over our heads. It didn't look as if she were in a hurry to go anywhere, but I put my hand on the cut end of her leash just in case.

"I should think Mrs. Livermore had such a big yard with a big fence that she could let the dog run loose right there and she'd get plenty of exercise," Bradford said. "It even says *Beware of Dog* on the gate. That's why I throw the paper through it."

"That's why no one would come in to deliver the milk or the mail or the groceries—"

"—or the paper," added Bradford. "Now I remember why the other boy quit. It was the dog, not just Mrs. Livermore."

"She tries to keep Kathy in her own smaller yard in the big yard," Ernie explained. "But it doesn't give her enough exercise, so Mrs. Livermore saw my ad for The Dog-Jog Service and this was a trial run. *Run!*" He groaned again.

"I think Kathy is very sweet," I said. "She's probably just enthusiastic. She must like you, Ernie, or she wouldn't have gone out willingly to walk with you."

"I wish she hated me," Ernie sighed. "It will be awful to go back and tell Mrs. Livermore that I won't walk her dog again. I'd already told her I charged by the size. I was going to get a minibike with the money."

Remember I told you ideas sort of took off in my head like a motor starting to rev up with a va-va-va-VA? I could feel it beginning to shudder in my head, when along came old Mr. Tilley, who works for Colonel Maypole except on Thursdays. It struck me right off as strange because I was sure it was Thursday. He had his straw hat set down tight on his head and a pair of overalls rolled up under his arm.

He looked at us and stopped. "Are you a disaster area?" he asked us.

"No," said Ernie, who was sitting up by then and picking the gravel out of his palms. My scratches were bleeding a little, but Bradford was all right, except for being cross about Mrs. Livermore and the paper and his bike, and that wasn't even bleeding, for silly's sakes.

But Kathy took one smell of Mr. Tilley and barked and growled and sprang to her feet and Mr. Tilley looked for the nearest tree to climb, and couldn't find one with a limb he could reach, so he stuffed his overalls in Kathy's jaws, and said, "There! You spoiled champeen. You ate my job, now you can eat my overalls—not me."

Kathy dropped the overalls. Then she lay down and used them for a pillow. So we all sat down beside her again, except Mr. Tilley, who was nervous.

"What do you mean, she ate your job?" I inquired. I hope you notice that "inquired." Reporters always inquire and I was already practicing for my career.

"I been moonlighting my Thursdays up at Mrs. Livermore's estate ever since Colonel Maypole decided to give me a day off a week. What do I need a day off a week to sit in my room in a boarding house for? The colonel thought I'd

like time to spend with my cronies. But they're all over at the cemetery now—"

"Working?" asked Bradford, not at all tactfully.

"Resting," said Mr. Tilley. "In peace. And I'm not about to join 'em yet. Not until I win the Sweepstakes once. So I answered Mrs. Livermore's ad for a gardener one day a week and made it Thursdays."

I stood there thinking that moonlighting in a garden sounded more like poetry than work. Until Mr. Tilley went on, "She's a terrible old woman. I could hear her screeching at me even over the sound of the mower I was riding and she fired me at the top of her lungs, she did. So now I'm on my way to see if Colonel Maypole won't let me work for him for free on my day off. Never was one jest to set and grow."

"But what did she fire you for?" asked Ernie. "What did you do?"

"I didn't do anything. I just wasn't looking when Kathleen Mavourneen Champeen jumped over her private fence and ate her way through Mrs. Livermore's Giant Multi-Hued Snapdragons that she was going to enter against Colonel Maypole's Baby Rainbow-Tinted Pincushion Dahlias for the Ladies' Garden Club Prize for Color in Border Plantings. That's all."

I was going to inquire how come Colonel Maypole competed in a Ladies' Garden Club competition, but then I realized there wasn't any Men's Garden Club and he had to do something with all those flowers in his hobbyhouse. If the flowers growing up each side of the front walk were what he was competing with, he'd be hard to beat.

"No wonder Mrs. Livermore was waiting by the gate so I'd get Kathy out of the yard for some exercise. Kathy must have been jet-propelled with all those flowers snap, crackle, popping inside her," said Ernie. "But I hate to take that dog back and face Mrs. Livermore. Do you suppose if I dropped that leash over her back and slapped her rump and said, 'Go home. Old Paint,' or something the way the wounded cowboy tells his horse to go home on TV, that Kathy'd wander back by herself? It sounds as if Mrs. Livermore'd still be standing there, breathing out fire."

Now I was already forming a picture of Mrs. Livermore in my mind. A snappish old lady who complained about the way her paper was folded and flung through her gate, and a weird old lady who fired a good gardener because *her* dog ate *her* prize flowers, and a scary old lady because she kept such a big dog you had to beware of.

"Breathing fire is right," said Mr. Tilley. "She's an old dragon, she is, and I'm through fighting her."

"So am I!" said Bradford Beeman.

"So am I!" said Ernie Tellerman.

And that puzzled me. "You mean you're all afraid of just an old lady?" I inquired.

"You take her the paper," said Bradford, and reached into the cloth bag on the back of his bike for a fresh copy of the *Maizefield Morning Star*. "And collect for last week while you're there. I saw her waiting for Ernie, with that dog leaning out over the iron fence, and I didn't even finish pushing my bike up the hill. Look—this is how she likes the paper folded, so it maybe won't fall apart when you fling it through the gate."

"You take Kathleen Mavourneen," said Ernie Tellerman, putting the cut end of her leash into my hand. "You can even have my pay for today."

"And good luck to you," said Mr. Tilley, and then he took off his hat and bowed to me.

Well, I said to myself, Georgina, it looks like you're stuck with the dragon.

"When you go by Mrs. Barberry's, tell my

sister Looey, who's playing in the yard with the kittens to tell my mother I won't be right back," I told Bradford, and then I said, "Come," to Kathleen and we walked down the sidewalk together.

Unfortunately that was just when Looey happened to be looking down the street and saw me and ran home and told my mother I was going away with a pony. So Bradford didn't see Looey and didn't think to knock on my door and speak to my mother direct, and when I didn't come back and didn't come back, my mother thought I might have been kidnaped by an itinerant photographer. She thought men still might be going around in these days with ponies and taking pictures in people's yards of kids sitting on a pony —like they did in the olden times of her youth— and some kid she knew wouldn't get off the pony and the photographer had gone away with her. She has a photograph of herself in a smocked silk dress from London, sitting on a pony and looking uncomfortable, and we all think it's funny but she doesn't. I could see me riding horseback in a silk smocked dress, for silly's sakes.

Anyway Kathleen and I got along fine and people and dogs we came to just got out of our way. I didn't even say "Heel," because if she got behind me and stumbled, she'd wipe me out. I figured side by side was better. I had the newspaper in my other hand, still folded up by Bradford. But the nearer I got to Mrs. Livermore's, the sweatier I got thinking about it, and the ink was beginning to rub off on me.

"Look," I said to Kathleen, "how would you like to take the *Maizefield Morning Star* to your mistress? Or are you the kind who eats up the news?"

Kathy bumped into me companionably enough, so I guess she liked to be talked to. But she didn't give me a clue about delivering the paper. The hill was getting steep and I was tempted to hang onto the leash and let her tow me. But in case Mrs. Livermore was watching, I thought it would be better to look in command. So we walked up to the front gate together. It had a black iron curlicued arch over the top, with two swinging sections below that latched shut in the middle, and when the latch stuck I had to put the paper down and use both hands to struggle with it.

Just then Kathy realized where she was and she didn't have Lassie's homing instincts. She wanted out—forever, I guess. I'd forgotten to tie the cut end of her leash into a loop to hang onto, so I just stood there, rattling the gate, and watching her leash fly by me like the end of a kite string rising up in the air. At the same time Mavourneen, Kathleen of Connacht's championship leap for freedom kicked up the loosely folded edition of the *Maizefield Morning Star,* and, helped by a gust of wind, distributed its pages like a flock of pigeons through the air, over the iron fence, and settled them down on the colorless borders of chewed greenery edging Mrs. Livermore's front walk.

"Kathleen!" I screamed, as I watched the wolfhound gallop down the hill we had just climbed up. "You're a bad girl!"

"And you are a shrill little girl," said a voice beside me that frightened me so I nearly—well, you can guess what I nearly. But I didn't. I just slowly unfroze my neck and turned enough to see who spoke, and there was the dragon, Mrs. Winchendon Livermore herself, breathing noisily through her highly arched nostrils, her chest rising and falling in beastly heaves, and I stood there waiting to be scorched by her wrath like Bradford Beeman and Mr. Tilley and poor Ernie Tellerman would have been if I hadn't been brave enough to take their places.

That gave me courage, because I added that up as one ten-year-old female taking the place of two eleven-year-old males plus one who was

maybe eighty or ninety. It's hard to tell a man's age once he's older than you know your own father is.

So when Mrs. Winchendon Livermore asked, "Just what do you think you're doing?" only she made it sound like a scream in a bad dream instead of a reasonable question, I said, "Bringing you the *Maizefield Morning Star* for Bradford Beeman, and returning your Irish wolfhound for Ernest Tellerman, and telling you that Mr. Tilley was moonlighting in your garden on Thursday just so he wouldn't be lonely."

"Moonlighting in my garden? In broad daylight? What do you mean?"

"Moonlighting is when someone has two jobs," I explained. I knew, because when my mother wanted to go back to work last year my father said, "If there's any moonlighting to be done in this family in order to get all these girls married off or through college, I'll do it. You should be home, taking care of them." And I said to Mother, "Isn't that romantic of Daddy to want to work for us somewhere in the moonlight," and she said, "That's not being romantic. That's being foolish and stubborn. All moonlighting means is working more than one job. And *I* would love a change from all this housework."

40

But Mrs. Winchendon Livermore was still firing questions at me. "And where else did Mr. Tilley work, may I ask? He didn't mention any other place to me."

"He works every day but Thursdays for Colonel Maypole."

"The colonel? My chief competitor? No wonder Mr. Tilley let Kathleen eat the snapdragons. It was sabotage!"

Her eyebrows arched even more than her nostrils and sort of drew her glittering glasses up higher on her face so they glared worse than her eyes. I wondered if her hands would be tough and scrawny and scaly when she took them out from behind her back. I began to wonder what she was holding up against her back. A walking cane? A hunting rifle? A dragon's tail?

"No wonder when I asked Mr. Tilley what he was going to do to replace the flowers before the Garden Day competition next week, all he could say was 'Put in potted petunias.' Never! A Livermore would never stoop to potted petunias. I think Colonel Maypole must have been in a plot with him. A potted petunia plot."

She looked disdainfully over at the chewed-up bed, where the *Maizefield Morning Star* pages were flapping about among the beheaded flower stalks, and I said practically, "Too bad

you can't use paper flowers. The *Morning Star* makes enormous ones."

"The *Morning Star* does what?"

It made me nervous the way she repeated what I said, making a big fuss out of something you just said to say something. It kept me busy explaining myself and other people, and she hadn't given me a chance yet to say that I knew Mr. Tilley felt awful about the snapdragons and I knew he couldn't be plotting with Colonel Maypole. They were both nice men. But she was waiting for me to explain about her newspaper.

"We make flowers out of the *Star* sometimes. On rainy days. When there's nothing else to do. Flowers and hats and birds and animals. You just fold them about a bit. My sister Cynthia made a lot of flowers once and spray-painted them gold. The *Morning Star* is on tough newsprint. It's good for garbage, too," I said without thinking.

"Don't you ever *read* it?" asked Mrs. Livermore with a sniff.

"Some of it," I said honestly. "Like the movie ads and the Help Wanted and the funnies and the Advice to Teen-Agers, which sounds more like advice to calm parents than help kids, and the Ladies' Page when Christine announced her engagement. Why?" I decided to inquire.

"You used the word newsprint for paper. Most girls your age wouldn't say that."

I shrugged. "I worked on our school paper, and our class did a unit on ecology. Do you know how many trees it takes to put out the Sunday edition of the *New York Times?* It's stupendous! Or one week of even the *Maizefield Morning Star?*"

"Do you?"

"I did when we wrote our reports, but I couldn't quote accurately right now without looking it up. I'm going to be a reporter, so I believe in getting my facts straight. But you ought to have a collection system for old *Morning Stars* and recycle your paper."

"*I* should?"

"Bradford Beeman said you owned the paper. You told him you'd have him fired if he didn't keep delivering it."

"You're not only shrill, you are *brash,*" said Mrs. Livermore. "I don't know how your mother puts up with you."

"Because she has five other girls, so she's used to it," I said. "It's my father who suffers most. He doesn't like us to tell him what to do."

"No one likes to be told what to do anymore,"

said Mrs. Livermore, breathing hard again. "No one! No one knows how to take orders and no one knows how to get anything done efficiently without taking a few sometimes in his life. Because if you don't learn to order yourself, you can't give orders to others." Then she almost scared me into taking off like a rocket by swinging her hand from behind her back with a pitchfork in it, and I thought she was aiming it right at me.

"Well, you can make yourself useful now you've brought me the paper," she said. "You can pick it up while I spade up those flower beds."

She stood there, waving the pitchfork in the direction of the flower beds, and I took about seven scared giant steps and bent over to gather up the *Maizefield Morning Star,* all the time not quite sure but what she'd give me a prod in the rear. It was a big edition of the paper because the supermarkets all ran their ads on Thursdays and there were a lot of pages strewn around. I thought from the frantic way Mrs. Livermore had looked that she'd be already heaving that dirt over in the flower beds but instead she was leaning on the pitchfork and thinking.

When I got the pages all picked up, I took

time to smooth them out and put them in order and carried the paper over to her, with the pink tabloid-size shopping extra on top. "'Shall I put this up on your front porch where it won't blow around?"

"That sounds sensible." She frowned down at me. "Tell me, are you used to figuring things out, making suggestions, and doing things for yourself, as well as being able to do what you're told?"

"It's the only way you can survive when you have five sisters," I told her.

"I see. What's your name?"

"Georgina Poindexter Farraday Gooch." I decided to give her the whole business. "I was named for my great-grandmother who is going to be commemorated on a stamp next month, and I'm trying to earn enough money to go and represent the family at the ceremonies. So I'm job-hunting and if you don't mind, I'd like to get on with it. I just brought back the dog and the paper as a favor for two friends."

I thought when I mentioned *the dog,* she'd get upset about where Mavourneen, Kathleen had gone off to all by herself. But for some reason my great-grandmother's name had taken her attention.

"My father told me about a Georgina Poindexter he knew back East who married a Far-raday and went west. She raised quite a ruckus out in one of those new states and got the women the right to vote long before the older part of the country followed along. Is that what your great-grandmother did?"

"Yes. In Boise, Idaho. She wrote VOTE IN BOISE FOR THE WOMAN'S VOICE—WOMEN ARE HERE FOR EVER."

"And some men better face it," said Mrs. Livermore, thrusting the pitchfork into the garden. "Especially Colonel Maypole. And to think I kindly and democratically allowed him to enter the Ladies' Garden Club. Do you happen to know, Georgina, what he's planning to compete with this year?"

"His front-walk borders. Mr. Tilley said they were plantings of Baby Rainbow-Tinted Pincushion Dahlias, and they are pretty."

"If you like that sort of fussy thing," snapped Mrs. Livermore. "The trouble is, he and Mr. Tilley can grow things so well it's hard for us women to compete with them."

"Then why did you let two men into your Ladies' Club?"

"Because I get awfully sick of just ladies," admitted Mrs. Livermore. "There's more petty bickering in some women's clubs than I can abide. But you see I was brought up in a man's world to do a man's job—so maybe I get impatient with unbusinesslike women."

"'What man's job?" I inquired, planning to take careful mental notes.

"My father was a managing editor of a newspaper. My mother died when I was four. So he took me all over the country, to wherever he had a job. Newspapermen move around a great deal. I always did my homework after school in the city room of whatever newspaper he was at. Then I married Winchendon Livermore, who owned and published nine newspapers. When he died ten years ago, I stayed here and sold all of them but the *Star*. I'm glad you at least approve of the paper it's printed on." She ended with either a snort or a sniff. It was hard to tell which, and she seemed to use them as punctuation.

I looked down at what I'd absent-mindedly been doing, and I'd been pleating up the top page of the pink shopping section the way Cynthia and I do to make paper flowers. You pleat them around in a fan and you can put about six or seven different-sized fans together and tape them onto a wire stem. Then you hack 'em up with scissors to fringe them and you've got like a fantastic chrysanthemum.

I was embarrassed and I blurted out, "You

could make a border of paper flowers and spray them all different colors. I'll bet Colonel Maypole and Mr. Tilley don't even know how to make paper flowers."

"Why should they?" asked Mrs. Livermore. "Boys usually sit around gluing model cars and airplanes together."

"You know what confuses me?" I asked, realizing that Mrs. Livermore hadn't led a typical housewifely life. "Why does everybody make a big thing out of it if you're a girl and you want to do a boy's-type job, or if you're a boy and you want to do a girl's-type job? Like Colonel Maypole and Mr. Tilley had to ask to get into the Ladies' Garden Club, and you say you had a man's job when you published a newspaper, and I can't get a job I want like mowing lawns or trimming hedges, but I can get a job I don't want like baby-sitting or cleaning bathrooms."

"Georgina, let's go up on the porch and have a cold glass of grapefruit punch and a talk," said Mrs. Livermore. She pronged the pitchfork more firmly into place and I followed meekly, carrying the newspaper. I wondered what Bradford Beeman and Ernie Tellerman and Mr. Tilley would say if they knew the dragon had invited me to sit down for a punch and a talk.

But just at that point she heard her phone

inside the mansion ringing like crazy, and apparently there was no one to answer it but her. So she stalked along quickly and motioned me to follow her inside, and she went to an alcove under the enormous staircase that wound around a hall that was three stories high, and answered the telephone.

"Indeed," she said. "Well, I am sorry to hear that. Yes, I agree. It's a major catastrophe for you, Colonel. I'll have a taxi pick her up as soon as possible, if you can manage to hold onto her until I can get one. My car is out of commission."

She hung up and I thought I saw a smile trying to win out over her stern face. "Our talk will have to wait, Georgina. That was Colonel Maypole. I must say I always knew Champion Mavourneen, Kathleen of Connacht was a highly intelligent dog. When you let her go, do you know what she did? She went back to find the boy who started out with her and it seems he was lying on the colonel's front lawn with a friend and they were watching Tom Tilley weed the borders of Baby Rainbow-Tinted Pincushion Dahlias, and well, there's just something about Tilley that Kathy doesn't appreciate. Not since he turned the hose on her one day when she was frisky. So she just decided to lie down and rest

too—in the flowers. And to roll around and scratch her back on the Pincushion Dahlias, and it seems she's crushed and scratched up about as many flowers down there as she ate up here! Oh, Kathy is a most intelligent dog."

And at that point Mrs. Winchendon Livermore began to laugh. She laughed so hard she had to sit down on the grand staircase and hold onto her sides until the tears came into her eyes and she had to fumble around in the bosom of her dress for a lace handkerchief. Remember in the fairy stories, where the wicked witch cries and washes herself away to a puddle on the floor? Or the dragon gets tickled and laughs until all its scales fall off clank, clank, clank—and there is a human being that's been imprisoned under the armor plate?

I wondered if Mrs. Winchendon Livermore was going to cascade down the stairs into a laughing waterfall, or suddenly break out in a curly wig and clown make-up. I didn't know what to expect—except to hope she didn't laugh herself to pieces before it was too late.

So to bring her back to reality, I inquired, "Do you live here all by yourself, Mrs. Livermore?"

She nodded and tried to stop laughing. She even grabbed the banisters and pulled herself up. Then she gestured up at all the empty space in the three-storied hall with its crystal chandelier dull and dust-dimmed. Through the open doorway into a formal drawing room I could see that most of the furniture looked worn and a corner of one of the rugs was chewed. There were hundreds of copies of the *Star* piled on chairs. She could have started a recycling bin right there.

"Isn't it fantastic?" asked Mrs. Livermore. "All this huge house, and Kathy and I are the only ones in it. That's why I bought the biggest dog I could find. I can let her loose in a room and after two minutes it will look as if thirty people had just left after a party. She can clear a tabletop with a sweep of her tail and move the objet d'art on a mantelpiece with a front paw, if she wants to. She keeps me busy cleaning up, as if I still had lots of friends coming and going the way it was when Winchie was alive."

I thought that was pretty sad, when you had to get the biggest dog in the world to make up for people not being around. But Mrs. Livermore had turned into such a huffy dragon the last few years, I guess she'd scared all her old friends away.

"What made you turn into a dragon?" I asked, and then when I heard myself ask it, I just stood there, expecting her to rekindle herself and start snorting and ranting again. Notice I *asked*. It was a question that just popped out from me, Georgie, not from Georgina Gooch, reporter at large.

"Oh, my!" gasped Mrs. Winchendon Livermore, and she sank back on the staircase again, looking like a faded roll of silk that would sigh and slither down the stairs any second. "What made me turn into a dragon?" she whispered. "Is that what people have been thinking all these years—Old Lady Livermore is a dragon? While I've been thinking, 'Henrietta, you can't let anyone know you're afraid. Or lonely. You have to be brave, efficient, forceful Mrs. Winchenden Livermore for the rest of your life.' Why, I'm the only president that the Maizefield Ladies Garden Club has ever had, and I always thought it was because they knew I could do it better than anyone else. But maybe it was because no one was brave enough to tell me to stop! You see, Georgina, when Winchie died, I thought any sensible woman could pick up the pieces and be self-sufficient and independent and useful all by herself—a self-contained individual. But I guess all through our lives we need other people close to us—all kinds of people. Men, women, and children. We all need each other."

I heard what she said all right, and I suppose some day when I've lived longer and figured out more things for myself I'll remember her sitting on the stairs and whispering in a wavy silky voice about people needing each other just as much as they need to be individuals. But right then it was still an uncomfortable situation and I didn't know how to get out of it. Then I remembered she'd said she'd send a taxi to pick up Kathy at Colonel Maypole's, and I wondered how a taxi driver would like Kathy for a passenger in either the front seat or the back. Especially if it was a man who was afraid of dogs.

So I asked, "Would you like me to run down to Colonel Maypole's and see Ernie and together we'll bring Kathy back? He really wanted to be paid for today's Dog-Jog, but maybe he'd split it with me and as I said, I'm job-hunting and I need the money, too."

"All right," said Mrs. Livermore. "Whatever you say."

"Then don't call a taxi and we'll be back."

Halfway down the steep hill I thought, "That was dumb!" Neither Ernie nor I would enjoy climbing that hill again on a hot day, especially if we had to drag Kathy. I should have let her send a taxi for all of us. But the rest of the time, I was thinking about Mrs. Livermore and how her name was Henrietta—just as second-hand as Georgina—and how she'd lost all her friends from being so independent and prickly-dragon.

I forgot all about the fact I'd just been sent out to mail a letter and take my little sister Looey for a walk. And I didn't know my mother was already sending my sisters scouting around our neighborhood looking for me, for silly's sakes. I'd only been gone for two hours. But my mother had gotten that stupid idea in her head from Looey, who didn't know a big dog from a pony, that I'd been kidnaped by an itinerant photographer who used a pony as a lure. Even if they still had photographers around like that, wouldn't you think my mother'd give me—a ten-year-old girl who was going to fly alone to Boise, Idaho—me, the great-grand-daughter of Georgina Poindexter Farraday—credit for more sense than that? Sometimes I wonder what she got out of studying rat psychology anyway!

Colonel Maypole was still shuddering over his crushed borders, mainly because Kathy was still crushing them, when I got there. She was as relaxed as Ferdinand smelling the flowers, and stretched out motionless among them. No one had dared to tell her to move. The colonel and Mr. Tilley were trying to estimate how many Pincushion Dahlias it would take to replace her recumbent yardage and Bradford Beeman and Ernie Tellerman were still recovering from their own shocks by lying on the lawn. It looked like I'd left them playing Still Pond No More Moving.

"And this was the year I was sure I could beat that woman at her own game," mourned Colonel Maypole as I went and stood silently beside him. "Oddly enough that woman can grow things so well even without a gardener—after all, Mr. Tilley had only helped her out a few times—that she's hard for us men to compete with."

"If it's hard to compete with a lady, then why did you ask to join the Ladies' Garden Club?" I inquired.

"Because I thought I could beat a woman," said Colonel Maypole. "That's why. But I guess the old saying's true. You can never win with any woman. Not even a—dog," he finished politely, suddenly conscious of my female undefiled mind. By the way, I hope you realize that I like words—especially interesting-sounding

ones like that recumbent back there, and un-de-filed.

Kathy twitched her ears when he said "dog," and that reminded me of what I had come for. Kathy.

"Come!" I said to her, and she didn't move.

"Go!" begged Colonel Maypole, but that didn't work either.

"Move!" I tried again. "Kathy, I told Mrs. Livermore that Ernie and I would bring you back."

"What did you say that for?" Ernie groaned, moving only his lips.

"Because I thought it would be easier to do it together," I admitted. "And she said she'd pay us both. Come on, Ernie. I tried to help you out. Now you can help me. And she's not really a dragon at all. She's just a lonely old woman."

Then my mind began to race, with a very faint and gentle v-v-v-v . . . just a hint of an idea so fragile that really revving up on it might choke it completely.

"Colonel Maypole, I think Mrs. Livermore would appreciate your advice on what to put in her garden."

"My advice! Are you crazy?" For a minute I thought the colonel could have been an old dragon on his job, too. His look burned right through me.

"She didn't exactly take kindly to Mr. Tilley's suggestion of potted petunias. I thought you might have another idea."

"Potted petunias? What made you think of that, Tom? The fact that my greenhouse is full of potted petunias?"

"I thought you could spare a few," said Mr. Tilley. "They overdid themselves this year."

"True," said Colonel Maypole. "Odd colors, too. But if I gave them to her, what would I use to replace my Baby Rainbow-Tinted Pincushion Dahlias?"

"Since you have so many petunias, why don't you both use the same thing?" I asked.

"And have my borders look exactly like hers? Then neither of us would win."

"That's right," I said. "It would give some other lady—or rather, some other gardener—a chance to win for a change. I gather Mrs. Livermore has had a monopoly, and sorry as she is about your flowers, she thinks maybe it would be a good time for someone else to win the prize, as well as run the club."

"But where would not winning leave me?" asked the colonel indignantly.

"It would leave you being a complete gentle-

man and likely the next president of the Ladies' Garden Club," I suggested before I realized I hadn't made the suggestion to Mrs. Livermore yet.

"Being a complete gentleman!" harrumphed Colonel Maypole. "That's rather an impossibility now that women have taken over everything." But I could see him meditating on the other part of my sentence.

"It would make me very happy," said Mr. Tilley, "if we could give her some of your petunias. I jest don't like to see any woman suffering from loneliness as much as she is. It isn't right."

"She had to buy Kathy for a companion," I explained to the colonel. "She needs a lot of activity around her to keep her cheerful."

It was strange, I realized then, what made different people cheerful. My mother said sanity and cheerfulness could only be preserved if the house was completely empty—except for her— at least once a day. Even for ten minutes.

Just then Kathy arose, and I had the presence of mind to grab the end of her leash. She must have been thinking as she lay there in the flowers. Maybe, if she was as intelligent as Mrs. Winchendon Livermore claimed, she'd figured out that after her first mistake at home, she'd have to ruin the colonel's flowers to get herself back into the dragon's good graces. So having done it, she could now return and be pampered.

"Bring the petunias!" I reminded them. Ernie said he had to go jog some other dogs, it was so late, and I really was more than welcome to Kathy. So I struggled to keep my balance while Kathy bounded along the street and back up the hill. My arms were about out of their sockets from holding onto her when we reached the top.

I looked back hopefully, though, as I wanted some company when I faced Mrs. Livermore again. It wouldn't be easy to propose that Colonel Maypole become president of the Ladies'

Garden Club. But not a creature was stirring all the way up the hill, except far off in the distance a police car was slowly patrolling the street. It stopped and an officer got out and went up the front walk to a house.

But Kathy wasn't looking back. She dashed on through the open gate and into the yard and up to the front porch where, to my amazement, Mrs. Livermore was trying to pleat a paper flower fan out of the *Maizefield Morning Star.*

"Hello, Kathy. Just lie down like a good little girl." Kathy did. There was no doubt that Mrs. Livermore had an awesome way about her. "Georgina, you'll have to show me how to wire these things onto a stem. I've decided to attempt a little humor. I'll make a border planting out of the *Star.*"

"What if it rains?" I worried, thinking horridly of a competition viewing of rusting wires topped by wet newspaper pulp.

"It won't," she said confidently.

If that was how she'd made up her mind, and she hadn't liked Mr. Tilley suggesting the potted petunias anyway, what would she do if and when they arrived bearing plants? I put all my mental potential into negative thought waves to Colonel Maypole. *Don't bring potted plants. Forget the whole thing.*

"You need some florist's tape or florist's wire to bind the paper to the stems," I told her.

"I don't think I have any on hand," she said. "I've never gone in for corsages. Flowers should be planted or arranged. But not worn."

She certainly had her opinions, didn't she? And she gave a sniff to emphasize that one.

But I felt in my shirt pocket and came up with two rubber bands—one yellow and one red. Sometimes the only way I can remember not to chew on my long hair is to braid it, so I keep rubber bands everywhere. They are also good to chew on.

I cut the bands with her scissors and then went and got a green wire plant stake from the decimated garden. She held it while I tried to wind the rubber bands around over the paper and then tie them on the stick. It wasn't easy. Rubber bands stretch and then snap out of your hands just as you're tying them. I got a little uptight about it, particularly since it was my idea.

"Are you sure you want to use paper flowers?" I asked.

"It's an excellent idea. It will neatly remove me from the competition, which I don't mind now that I know that Colonel Maypole is out of it, too. Although I would have liked to beat a man at his own game. And it will make very good publicity for both the *Star* and the Ladies' Garden Club. We always have a staff photographer go along for the competition viewing."

"But Colonel Maypole may end up with a border after all. He says he's going to put in potted petunias."

"He is! And I thought he had good taste."

"I guess he likes potted petunias. He has a whole greenhouseful. In fact—" I tried frantically to think of how to prepare her to receive the potted plants, should they unfortunately arrive. "Do you know what would be a real surprise? You could ask Colonel Maypole for some of the petunias and I'd spy for you and see how he puts his in. You could put yours in the same way, and then you'd cancel each other out and some other person could win the prize this year. And no one but me would know you'd arranged the whole thing that way—so some of the other people could make a name for themselves in the Garden Club."

"Georgie, you aren't clever. You're devious!" she said. That was a new one on me and I'd have to look it up and I couldn't even tell from her voice whether she said it with relish because it was bad to be devious or not. But perhaps if she had the idea of asking him for plants and he arrived with some, she'd feel great. She could accept them graciously without being embarrassed about having to ask for them.

"But would he let me have some plants?" she wondered.

"Possibly," I said. "I know he has the best interests of the Ladies' Garden Club at heart. He wanted a really keen competition this year. Actually, he'd make a good president, he is so enthusiastic."

I threw that line in as quickly as possibly as if it were too preposterous even to think about.

But Mrs. Livermore was as stunned by the idea of a man as president as I'd been to read somewhere lately about a lady wanting to play pro football. I mean, I can see a girl my age who's good at sports wanting to play Little League with the boys. But having a guy as big as Rosie Greer fall on you on a frozen football field, for silly's sakes! That's senseless! And Maizefield is a town that won't even accept a lady school-bus driver, even though everyone knows mothers have the best training for it. They know instinctively when the noise has reached the point to yell, "That's it! Everybody shut up now—or we'll all get killed."

The yellow rubber band flipped out of my hands one last time. Mrs. Livermore lost her

grip on the fans of paper, and the *Star* flower popped apart and fell just like litter on the porch.

I found myself giving a disgusted snort just like Mrs. Livermore's.

And then the gate swung open and I'd swear it was a parade rolling into the yard. It had everything but a band. It had a station wagon so loaded with flowers that it looked like a Miss America float, except that Colonel Maypole was driving, with Mr. Tilley as the one in back surrounded by Passion Purple, Lavish Lavender, and Pettable Pink-Frilled Petunias.

It had Bradford Beeman on his bicycle. It had Ernie Tellerman having psyched himself up for another Dog-Jog so he seemed surrounded by barking dogs, even though he was only jogging one poodle, one schipperke, one dachshund, and one Norwegian elkhound. With the leashes weaving about, he looked more like a maypole

70

than the colonel. It had the police patrol car, with my mother looking worried, holding Looey on her lap, sitting next to a policeman. And it was followed by my father's company's pickup truck, which he must have borrowed after an emergency call from my mother. It has *The Expert Exterminating Company* scrolled in yellow letters on the green doors. When I saw him driving it, I wondered for the first time in my whole life why my mother, the rat psychologist, had married a man who ended up in the bug-and-pest-control business! It must have been a real compelling magnetic attraction after all—much more fatefully romantic than I'd ever realized. But there he was driving and looking so upset and hungry that I knew it must be his lunch hour, and Christine, Cheryl, Cynthia, and Charlene were in the back. They were still calling, "Georgie! Answer us, Georgie!" when they pulled into the driveway.

Who needed a band?

Mrs. Livermore stood like a queenly reception committee of one on the front porch, the garden stake still in her hand like a scepter.

"Georgie!" My mother jumped out of the police car and gave me such a hug you wouldn't even have thought she had five other girls. "We thought you were kidnaped."

"Where's the pony?" asked Looey, the dumb kid who started it all. Kathy looked at her in disgust, and didn't even get up to lick her.

"We've also got a complaint about a vicious dog, Mrs. Livermore," began the police officer. But he faltered when Mrs. Livermore began to turn from queenly gracious to dragonly prickly right before his eyes. As for Kathy, she let out an enormous gusty sigh that set the newspaper flowers to fluttering around her and then closed her eyes on the whole scene.

"Who made the complaint, may I inquire?" asked Mrs. Livermore. But it sounded like the question of a Supreme Court judge, not a reporter.

"I did," admitted Colonel Maypole, arriving with a Lavish Lavender Potted Petunia in his left hand and a Passion Purple one in his right. Mr. Tilley was right behind him carrying two Pettable Pinks. "But I drop the charge. We come, Tilley and I, bearing gifts and saying, *Peace!*"

I must say, when the colonel wanted to he could be as dramatic as Mrs. Livermore.

My father and sisters and Bradford Beeman and his bike and Ernie Tellerman and his dogs all clustered as close as they could, and I almost yelled, "Duck! Throw yourselves in the nearest ditch. She's going to breathe out flames of fire!"

But it must have looked to her like the makings of the first party she could give since her husband died. She changed from queen to dragon to hostess all with the tilt of her eyebrows and the help of a smile. I couldn't believe it when I heard her admiring the potted petunias.

"Colonel Maypole! Mr. Tilley! How very generous of you. Those blooms are—really blooming! Do come in. And Georgina's mother, Mrs. Gooch, how charming to meet you. You have one of the most intelligent girls I've ever met. Georgina is very refreshing. Do come in. And Georgina's sisters—you must be very fond of Georgina to drop everything and hunt for her. Do come in. Mr. Gooch, what a pleasure to meet such a handsome man. How very, very proud you must be of your whole family. Not many men are privileged to have such loving daughters—and you must be especially proud of the one who is about to travel to represent you all in Boise, Idaho. There are sandwiches on the mantelpiece in the living room. I made them while Georgina fetched Kathy. And a large bowl of grapefruit punch. Do come in. Boys! Inside—but leave the dogs and the bike here, please. And you, Officer? A liverwurst and bacon sandwich? A glass of punch?"

"I never eat or drink on duty, ma'am," the officer said quickly. "As long as everything is all right I'll just ride along." He shook his head after all the people who'd disappeared into the house. "But imagine thinking a girl as big as this one here could be kidnaped by a pony or that you had a vicious dog, Mrs. Livermore! Pretty silly, isn't it!"

Kathy, however, wasn't going to be dismissed as silly and she rose up in one swoop and put her paws on the officer's shoulders, so she was eye to eye with him. Or rather, eye to goggle, because the officer shut his eyes in horror, leaving just his dark goggles to stare Kathy down. But Kathy wasn't vicious. She just wiped his nose with her tongue, and removed her paws suddenly, which left him teetering backward and flailing his arms for balance. Mrs. Livermore caught him by one hand and I by the other, and we helped him into his patrol car.

74

He drove out quite quickly for a dazed man.

When we went into the house, the living room did look like a party, with people standing about munching the liverwurst and bacon sandwiches and marveling at the tremendous crystal punch bowl that looked big enough to swim in.

My father was happily talking caterpillars and cutworms with Colonel Maypole, and my mother was inviting Mr. Tilley to supper on any Thursday night he felt lonely, and offering him Looey to take to the zoo any Sunday. For a walk, of course. It all sounded like a party, too.

Mrs. Livermore hostessed her way from one person to another, even including Bradford Beeman and Ernie Tellerman. She sympathized with Christine over her no-pop-up toaster and the fact that one of her sisters could not be in her wedding party due to other plans. "But I would be delighted to attend your wedding," I heard her say. "Perhaps you'd even like to have your reception here. It's such a big place—and we certainly could make it like an enormous conservatory full of potted petunias."

I could see that Mrs. Livermore had gotten carried away and could easily take command of a situation even better than Cheryl and in a much more overwhelming way.

But Christine stood up to her. "Thank you,

but the plans are all made, except I would love to have you come to the wedding."

Then my father came up to her and said, "I must be getting back, Mrs. Livermore. There's no rest for weary exterminators you know! Something's always bugging us, ha-ha."

"In a moment, Mr. Gooch. Do sit down, everyone." She stood by the mantelpiece and everyone hastily scrambled for seats, some just perching on the piles of newspapers already huddled on the chairs. Kathy wandered in from outside and took up almost a whole rug. The dogs left outside were barking and making a commotion like people who couldn't buy tickets to get in. Mrs. Livermore cleared her throat and I thought for a minute she was going to say, "Will the meeting please come to order."

"Just a little business that we all can solve together," she announced. "It has come to my attention, through Georgina here, that I have been neglecting a civic duty. And I don't mean the Ladies' Garden Club—which, now that we have two fine men supporting it, one of whom may run for president, I understand, and if he does he will surely be elected, we should rename as the Maizefield Garden Club, open to all men and women, and I shall propose this at the very next meeting. But I mean my civic duty as to recycling newspapers—namely, of course, the *Maizefield Morning Star*. Now it has also come to my attention that Georgina, who has the honor of representing *women,* as well as her own family, at the Georgina Poindexter Farraday Commemorative Stamp Issue First-Day Ceremonies in Boise, Idaho, on Friday the twentieth is trying to earn enough money to make the trip."

My father looked uncomfortable, as if he'd been caught being an ogre. But Mrs. Livermore saved the scene neatly by saying, "Of course, any father of a bride would find it hard to finance a wedding and a plane trip at the same time. Anyway, I've decided to start a business, and I thought we could all incorporate a little company together. Now it will take a consultant and manager, and Mrs. Gooch, you have such excellent business experience—"

"Now just a minute," said my father. "My wife, Eve, may have been to college, and for five months she was a psychologist practicing on rats. But business experience! You need a man to run a company."

"I need someone who is used to budgeting, bookkeeping, preparing tax forms, writing letters, buying products, keeping cars and machines in repair, planning efficient schedules, talking to personnel, arbitrating disputes, and working long hours," Mrs. Livermore recited.

"Exactly," said my father. "It's a man's job. And I'm sorry, Mrs. Livermore, but I already have a job, and Eve doesn't have that kind of experience at all."

"But your wife has the perfect qualifications, Mr. Gooch. Isn't she a good housekeeper and mother?"

"The best!" my father said hastily, but he said it proudly, too.

"Then she has had years of practice in keeping a weekly food budget, paying the bills, preparing tax forms—since you are such a busy man, of course—writing letters, shopping for products, keeping the family car running, keeping an efficient chauffeuring schedule to take six girls and herself to all the places they have to go, using her psychological talents to smooth family arguments, and working very, very long hours. She is eminently qualified."

"I accept," said my mother happily, even if she wasn't sure what she was accepting.

Despite his years of practice with all of us, my father couldn't get a word in edgewise. Mrs. Livermore went on. "Colonel Maypole, in your role with the armed forces, you were used to addressing the public, I'm sure."

"Well," hesitated the colonel, whose addresses had been largely the issuing of regulation orders —but he was flattered—"yes, I was."

"Then you shall be our publicity and liaison man—to seek out those who need our help and explain our services. Georgina, who is so articulate, can help you write publicity. The two of you will make a fine public relations team. *You* have years of experience with people and places. Georgina has energy, enthusiasm, and a good vocabulary. Nor is either of you easily intimidated."

"What about me?" asked Bradford Beeman, who hated to see a business being organized without his being able to earn some money toward his electronic computer set.

"And what about me?" asked Ernie, who'd have to walk dogs for years before he could afford a minibike.

"Hmmmm," said Mrs. Livermore, sizing up the rest of the unemployed. "We will need good strong workers. You boys and Cheryl, Cynthia, and Charlene will have to be the pickup and delivery detail for a while. Christine will be too busy getting married right now."

"Pickup and delivery of what, Mrs. Livermore?" I inquired.

"Why, delivery of the *Maizefield Morning*

Star, of course. Daily as now. And pickup weekly of all such used paper products—not excepting even the *New York Times.* We'll have a collection point—my six-car garage would do. There's only one car in it and that doesn't work. I think I'll turn it in for a truck." The thought positively inspired her. "I've always wanted to drive a truck—and now I can! Also, Mr. Tilley, we need you for research and development."

"For what?" asked Mr. Tilley.

"Thinking up things to do with newspapers besides recycling them to make more paper. Inventing, sort of."

"Oh," said Mr. Tilley, not too convinced.

"Like if you could pack wedding presents in shredded newspaper, maybe you could—mulch a garden with them!" suggested Christine with a brilliant smile.

"Or invent a solution you could dip newspapers in and then lay them over your driveway to resurface it," said my father. He looked surprised at hearing himself get into this unexpected conversation. But my father is basically a smart man, and I was glad to hear him taking part.

"Or how to fix leftover newspapers to eat somehow," said Bradford Beeman, reaching for a last sandwich that someone who didn't quite care for liverwurst and bacon had parked on a windowsill.

"You see," cried Mrs. Livermore happily, "what we can all do together! Mr. Gooch, perhaps Saturday you'd help me pick out a truck, and Georgie, I think if you started campaigning for our project, you could be as famous as your great-grandmother."

For once my father didn't groan. "I've been reconsidering your trip to Boise," he told me. "I guess I can find the money for your plane fare."

"And a new dress and a new suitcase," added my mother, who knew her budget limits.

"Yes—" sighed my father.

"You can work out those little details," said Mrs. Livermore. "The dress and the suitcase, that is. Georgina's trip will be paid for as a reporter for the *Star*. Anything as important as the Georgina Poindexter Farraday Commemorative Stamp Issue First-Day Ceremonies deserves a roving reporter."

So that's the story of how I didn't get to my own sister Christine's wedding, and Mrs. Winchendon Livermore did. And of how my father began to see his wife, Eve Merriweather Gooch, his daughters, and even his grandmother-in-law,

Georgina Poindexter Farraday, in a new light. And of how Colonel Maypole became president of the Garden Club and Mr. Tilley baby-sat Looey and two of her friends almost every Sunday at the zoo and talked the zoo keeper into a mulch of the Sunday *New York Times* mixed with the *Daily News* for the floor of the lion cub's cage.

I haven't heard how that's working out yet, because I just got back yesterday from a very exciting trip to Boise, Idaho, which you can read all about in the *Star* next week when I've recovered enough to write it up.

But it was a thrill, a positive thrill, when the bus arrived from the airport at Weedey's store on the main street in Maizefield to be met by the whole parade—Colonel Maypole and Mr. Tilley carrying flowers, a touching tribute picked from the only surviving Baby Rainbow-Tinted Pincushion Dahlias; Bradford Beeman waiting on his bike and Ernie leaning contentedly against Kathy after a good Dog-Jog through town; my mother and my sisters—except Christine who was off on her honeymoon—in the family station wagon; and most of all, my father, who stopped by even though it was his lunch hour. Believe me, that was much more reinforcing to my relationship with him than bowling with him ever would have been! And finally, Mrs. Livermore, leaning out of the cab of an enormous red truck filled with bundles of newspapers in the back. She was waving excitedly. She must have passed the Class 2 truck drivers' test she was worried about.

I was delighted to see that during the three days I'd been away, the company had at last agreed on a name and it was the one I'd suggested. Nobody had come up with a better one. There it was in huge gold letters on the door of the red truck—*The Paper Dragon*.

29771 MISHMASH, by Molly Cone. Illustrated by Leonard Shortall. Life is full of surprises for Pete when he gets Mishmash—a huge, black, friendly hound who turns the whole town topsy-turvy with his hilarious doings. (95¢)

29322 THE STREET OF THE FLOWER BOXES, by Peggy Mann. Illustrated by Pete Burchard. When Carlos decides to launch a campaign to sell window boxes, he becomes the center of all kinds of activities on his block. (60¢)

29309 DANNY DUNN *and the Smallifying Machine,* by Jay Williams and Raymond Abrashkin. Illustrated by Paul Sagsoorian. When Danny gets trapped in Professor Bullfinch's latest invention, he shrinks to insect size and must face survival in a world that has become a giant jungle. (60¢)

29759 THE MYSTERIOUS BENDER BONES, by Susan Meyers. Illustrated by Ib Ohlsson. When Kermit and Brian are hired to do a peculiar "odd job" on Bender Island, they get tangled up with a mysterious stranger in a wild and hilarious search for treasure. (95¢)

29334 GERTRUDE KLOPPENBERG (Private), by Ruth Hooker. Illustrated by Gloria Kamen. Trudy confides to her diary all her most private thoughts and feelings about the ups and downs in her life. (60¢)

29510 MAPLE STREET, by Nan Hayden Agle. Illustrated by Leonora E. Prince. Margaret Gage launches a campaign to have an ugly vacant lot made into a playground with swings, seesaws, grass, and flowers. (75¢)

29738 ENCYCLOPEDIA BROWN TRACKS THEM DOWN, by Donald J. Sobol. Illustrated by Leonard Shortall. See if you can keep pace with America's favorite super-sleuth as he tackles ten more hard-to-solve cases. (95¢)

29543 THE GHOST NEXT DOOR, by Wylly Folk St. John. Illustrated by Trina Schart Hyman. Strange signs of the existence of a ghost next door trigger the curiosity of Lindsey and Tammy who resolve to find out just what's happening. (75¢)

29323 NEXT DOOR TO XANADU, by Doris Orgel. Illustrated by Dale Payson. If she only had a best friend, Patricia was sure that she wouldn't care about being called Fatsy Patsy. Then a new girl moves into the apartment next door. (60¢)

29546 DRUGS AND YOU, by Arnold Madison. Illustrated with photographs. This straightforward account gives you basic information about the use and abuse of today's major drugs. (75¢)

(If your bookseller does not have the titles you want, you may order them by sending the retail price, plus 35¢ per book for postage and handling to: Mail Service Department, POCKET BOOKS, a division of Simon & Schuster, Inc., 1 West 39th Street, New York, N. Y. 10018. Please enclose check or money order—do not send cash.)

29642